George
and the
Dragonfly

READZONE
ReadZone Books Limited

First published in this edition 2015

© in this edition ReadZone Books Limited 2015
© in text Andy Blackford 2009
© in illustrations Sue Mason 2009

British Library Cataloguing in Publication Data (CIP) is available for this title.

Printed in Malta by Melita Press.

ISBN 978 1 78322 168 4

Visit our website: www.readzonebooks.com

George and the Dragonfly

Andy Blackford
and Sue Mason

READZONE

George watched a film about
lizards and snakes, and creatures
that slither in rivers and lakes.

6

He said to his mother, "Do you suppose, for my birthday or Christmas, I could have one of those?"

His mum shook her head.

"Most certainly not! You wanted a hamster and that's what you've got. It's me who looks after him, gives him his tea...

If you had a python, it's not hard
to see who'd have to feed him –
Daddy and me!"

"If I can't have a snake," said George to his hamster, "or a lizard or something, there's only one answer. I'll go to the jungle and live in the trees with a boa constrictor and six chimpanzees!"

So George packed a bag with some socks and some pants, and left for the Land of Man-Eating Ants.

But George had no sooner set foot in the garden, than a gorgeous green dragonfly said, "Beg your pardon! Before you go off and live in a tree, there's a couple of friends that I'd like you to see."

George followed the fly to where he was shown. Then, on its instructions, he lifted a stone.

There coiled a millipede, all shiny and black, and a bright orange beetle with stripes on its back.

George was amazed. They were brilliant and pretty – not what you'd expect in the midst of a city.

18

The dragonfly hovered and darted
beyond, and waited for George by
the side of a pond.

There were tadpoles and toads and a
fat friendly frog, and a great-crested
newt that lived under a log.

The dragonfly flew to a web on a shrub, where a red and green spider sat right at the hub.

Six of its legs were knitting a sweater,
while the two at the back were
writing a letter.

On a twig on a bush, the fly
landed next.

"I say! Do you mind?" said the twig,
clearly vexed.

"I'm an insect, you know – I just look like a stick!"

George was impressed.

"That's a brilliant trick!"

"Morning, young George!"
called a big bumble bee.
"Who needs a snake when
there's all this to see?"

But the dragonfly showed him one final surprise – a beautiful grass snake with beady black eyes.

29

"Thank you!" said George to
his dragonfly guide. "That was
totally great." And then he sighed.

"I think I'll go home and not live in that tree. Why go to the jungle when there's all this to see?"

Did you enjoy this book?

Look out for more *Swifts* titles –
stories in 500 words